MAID TO SERVE

Sissification, feminization
and an aristocratic mistress

Lady Alexa

Copyright © Lady Alexa 2021

All rights reserved. No reproduction, copy or transmission of this publication or section in this publication may be reproduced copied or transmitted without written permission of the author.

This novel is a work of fiction. Names, characters, businesses, places, events and incidents are either the products of the author's imagination or used in a fictitious manner. Any resemblance to actual persons, living or dead, or actual events is purely coincidental.

Contains explicit scenes of a sexual nature including forced male to female gender transformation, female domination, humiliation, spanking and reluctant feminisation. All characters in this story are aged 18 and over.

Strictly for adults aged 18 and over or the age of maturity in your country.

An early version of Maid To Serve appeared in Forced Feminization Bundle 3

Bundle 3 is no longer available and I have rewritten, updated and expanded Maid To Serve into this longer stand-alone novel.

RECEIVE DISCOUNTS AND SPECIAL OFFERS ON FORCED FEMINIZATION STORIES AND SEX TOYS

***Sign up to [Lady Alexa's Newsletter](www.ladyalexauk.com) from my website home page:
www.ladyalexauk.com***

CONTENTS

Chapter 1 – The Eccentric Aristocrat

Chapter 2 – An Unusual Housemaid

Chapter 3 – Ready for Her Ladyship

Chapter 4 – Her Ladyship's Rules

Chapter 5 – A Housemaid's Role

Chapter 6 – Show Respect

Chapter 7 – The Training Session

Chapter 8 – New Job New Clothes

Chapter 9 – A Pretty Tennis Skirt

Chapter 10 – The Housemaid Came

Chapter 11 – Foam Bath and Bubbles

Chapter 12 - A Shaved Sissy

Chapter 13 – The Great Release

Chapter 14 – The Grand Reveal

Chapter 1 – The Eccentric Aristocrat

Husbands can be such a pain. Ruth glared at David, threw her suitcase to the ground and stamped her foot into the gravel.

"We travel all day to get here and *now* you tell me you don't like the idea of being a servant to a rich lady?" She folded her arms across her chest. "This is what's going to happen, David."

David's eyes flowed over his still attractive wife. He loved the way her almost black hair waved and flowed after she washed it. OK, the colour needed a little help from a bottle these days and her curves were curvier than they used to be. Not a bad thing, he mused. Especially when she was riled. It had been her idea to do this and he hadn't had a lot of choice.

"You and I are going to go in there." She said, breaking him out of his daydream. She pointed to the building a hundred yards from where they were standing. Lady Elena Capel-Clifford's imposing country mansion rose like a living museum piece from a past era.

"You." He winced as her long sharp red nail stabbed through his shirt to his chest. "Will be respectful and we are going to be working for her as her servants whether you like it or not. "Ruth stabbed his chest again and put her head to one side. "Unless you have a better idea for how to get a job and a roof over our heads? Well, have you?"

David's eyes fell to the floor. "No Ruth." He glanced back up at her. He liked it when she was firm with his but wasn't about to admit that. He put his hands down to hide a hardening penis. If only she was like that more often; bossy, demanding. It was a fantasy to masturbate to, nothing more.

Ruth's hands were on her hips and she leant into his face. "No, I thought not. You know what? It's not my idea of fun either, but *needs must* and we need this so let's get on with it."

David looked down at the gravel, feeling like a schoolboy. His face flushed red at the thought and his erection grew. Ruth didn't get annoyed often. She was generally easygoing but, behind that façade, there was a strong lady. It's what he liked about her. When she got annoyed, it meant she was serious and it was best to go along with what she wanted. Like when she decided they would apply for this job. He'd have gone along with anything she wanted. If only she knew.

They grabbed the handles of their large suitcase and hitched the heavy brown holdalls over their shoulders. Their feet crunched along the gravel driveway to the mansion's front doors. *Needs must*, thought David, one of Ruth's sayings. There were others. Ruth stamped into the gravel harder than necessary; she'd calm down in a minute or two. Shame.

The suitcase wheels slid into the shingle, making parallel tracks. Sweat stuck to David's underarms beneath the late July sun. He saw sweat running down Ruth's rounded face, her black hair flat and lank in the thick summer humidity.

It had been a long journey and they caught their breath at the foot of a wide semi-circular stone staircase. It led up to the double-width entrance doors of the mansion. David took both suitcases and lifted their suitcases and lifted them step by step. He saw the look of relief on Ruth's face. Neither was getting any younger.

David stopped every couple of steps to plonk down the cases and take a rest. He stopped at the top of the steps to take a few deep breaths. David bent over in exhaustion, hands on his knees. The coo of a wood pigeon and the distant mew of a fox broke through the still air. They were ten miles from the nearest village. There was no traffic noise. That was weird.

The sun was setting behind low dark clouds across the horizon. The first spots of rain swirled in the heavy humid evening air; a storm promised to clear the thickness.

The last bus of the day had dropped them at the end of the long gravel driveway ten minutes ago with their suitcases.

Lady Elena's mansion and gardens occupied a central spot on one side of a small river in a verdant wooded valley. Ten acres of trees, bushes and lawns sat behind the massive three-story stone mansion. The front gardens were lawn and oak trees older than the house. The rustle of the shallow speedy river running over pebbles swished from behind the home.

Lady Elena had placed an advertisement with a nationwide employment agency for a couple to serve, clean, cook and maintain her gardens. It seemed a lot of work, but Ruth decided they had to apply. The positions came with free accommodation, food, uniform and a small salary. Lady Elena had explained on the Zoom interview they would be working with Candy, her current maid. They had giggled about that name afterwards. It was incongruous when compared to the stern aristocratic Lady Elena.

David had marvelled at her clipped aristocratic English accent. Her words had flown from the speaker like a sharpened javelin. She made the Queen sound common. Lady Elena said her previous gardener had left to work elsewhere and Candy couldn't manage everything on her own. Candy wasn't getting any younger. Lady Elena said she needed two live-in staff. A married couple was ideal.

David and Ruth had worked at the Welsh steelworks and been laid off three months previously. Cheap foreign steel imports were flooding in and the steel company could no longer compete. They'd had to rationalise. That was business double-speak for lay-offs. With the small Welsh town dependant on the steelworks, there was suddenly high unemployment and no prospects. Especially for a couple in their forties.

Once Ruth had found the job that came with accommodation and all food and bills included, she decided it was too good to ignore. Being little more than paid servants had not been their plan for life, but *needs must,* Ruth had said. She was always the practical one of the pair. And once she'd decided, David knew he had no choice. That was fine. It was a shame she didn't make more decisions, but that was the fantasy. Fantasies aren't real, they belong locked away in your head. Or when you're alone in the shower. Or when Ruth was out and you could go through her underwear drawer.

David had googled Lady Elena and found she was also in her mid-forties. Her photos showed her as slim and haughty with long silver hair. A face like a constipated trout, Ruth remarked. It was an observation confirmed on their Zoom call; when the connection wasn't freezing and dropping.

"The *Interwebby thingamabobby* is awfully slow out here in the countryside," Lady Elena had said, sounding as if she was sucking on a mouthful of pebbles.

There wasn't much about Lady Elena's life online. Unlike many aristocrats, she didn't frequent the events and social gatherings photographed for magazines. She had married an aristocrat called Lord James Capel-Clifford of Wye and Hereford. He used to sit in the House of Lords but stopped attending several years ago.

Before she married Lord James, she had been plain Elena Frankland. David and Ruth had not met Lord James on the Zoom call. The aristocratic couple's only daughter, nineteen-year-old Annabelle, had come into the picture at one point. She reminded her mother to remind us of our position in the hierarchy of society and in their home. The bottom rung.

Annabelle looked like a younger version of her mother although more buxom. Blonde rather than silver-haired.

Lady Elena had offered them the job following the Zoom interview. Ruth couldn't believe their luck. David was less sure but said nothing. Lady Elena had explained they would have their own double bedroom, an adjoining private bathroom and food and uniforms supplied. Her Ladyship said she had regular guests and insisted on a uniform. Annabelle had interjected off-screen that it was only right the servants dressed appropriately for their socially inferior position. Annabelle was going to be a pain, Ruth had said right after the interview. But *needs must*, she'd added

David and Ruth stood on the top step with the tall, bold mansion doors in front of them. They caught their breath before stepping into the unknown. A new life. David knew things were going to change. But would it be for the better, as Ruth believed? they'd soon find out.

Chapter 2 – An Unusual Housemaid

David pressed the round brass door button to the right of the large polished oak front doors. A ringing sound echoed from behind the entrance. The sun was setting and an inky darkness descended around them. They waited several minutes.

The doors swung open and a tall slim middle-aged woman with a vast amount of long blond hair faced them. It was thick and flowed over her shoulders and down to the nape of her back. David gaped at her heavily made-up face. The woman wore a short black housemaid's dress. She moved to one side and motioned them to enter with a wave of one hand. Her long pink fingernails were not what David expected on a servant at an aristocrat's mansion.

"Hello, you must be Mrs and Mr Davies. I'm Candy." She looked to the floor and dipped at the knee.

David noted the unusual reversal of Mrs and Mr and that her maid's dress was far too short for someone of her age. It flared out from a high narrow waist below enormous breasts. The dress front was low-cut and mountains of flesh spilt over, seemingly about to pop out at any moment. White starched petticoats held her dress out like a ballerina's skirt; voluminous undergarment formed an ostentatious frill around the bottom of the dress. She had a small white apron tried to the front. The dress didn't cover her black stocking tops and David gaped down at the garter straps clasped to them.

David and Ruth walked past Candy and into the hallway. Portraits of ancient stern ancestral male faces stared out from dark paintings along the length of the wide passage. Candy was two or three inches taller than David. She might have been pretty under her heavy make-up, long black false eyelashes, thick bottle-blond hair and bright red lipstick. David closed his mouth.

Ruth cleared her throat. She seemed to be recovering from the unexpected style of the housemaid. "Hello Candy. Please. Call me Ruth"

"Yes, Madam Ruth." Candy's voice was high, forced and as posh as her employer's but without the authority. She dipped her head and made a small curtsey to Ruth.

David watched Ruth's forehead crease in surprise at Candy's appearance; it was like something out of an online fetish video. Not that Ruth would know about that, he only looked at them when she was out and always made sure he cleared the history. Ruth would not have approved.

Lady Elena had said she expected them to wear uniforms. Her email explained they were to be black trousers and a white shirt or blouse for serving and cleaning. She would provide something more suitable for gardening. She had asked for their measurements by return email so she could have their uniforms ready. The idea of wearing a maid's dress like Candy's flashed through David's mind and he squashed it away.

He mentally added that idea to his shower fantasy.

Ruth wasn't concerned by the idea of them wearing matching black trouser uniforms. He hated the idea but Ruth told him it would be like wearing the steel company's overalls. Ruth, the practical one as ever. At least they wouldn't need to buy much clothing. That would be a bonus considering their current financial situation.

"Please follow me, Ms Davies and David," Candy said through the same virtual mouthful of pebbles as her employer. She turned smoothly on her high heels; they presented no problem for her. Clearly, she'd been wearing heels for some time.

"Why did she say *Ms Davies* and *David*?" David whispered into his wife's ear. She shrugged.

"Candy, I said you could call me Ruth," Ruth said. "And my husband is David."

"Of course, Madam Ruth." Candy said.

Ruth shrugged at David and they followed Candy along the hallway, her heels clicking like shotgun pellets against a tin can. Candy walked like a graceful gazelle, considering her height. She took one small step in front of the other, her small flat bottom wiggling side to side. She stopped at the bottom of a flight of double-width stairs that circled up the next floor. A swirling dark wood bannister flowed upstairs like a smooth brown serpent.

"I will show you to your bedroom, Madam Ruth and David." Candy glanced back at Ruth then David and dropped her long false eyelashes provocatively at him. David saw Ruth glare from the side of his vision. Candy's brief sensual glance had not been his imagination.

"Lady Elena will make your acquaintance once you've prepared yourselves. It wouldn't be appropriate for you to be meet Her Ladyship in your current state. She has high standards."

Candy turned and led them up the double-width staircase. Her frilly panty-clad bottom was exposed as David looked up. David struggled behind with their two large suitcases, his eyes running over Candy's legs. Ruth strained with the holdall bags. Candy led them from the ground floor, past the 1st floor and up to the 2nd floor.

She took them along a dark corridor lined with mahogany panels and with a deep brown floor carpet. Candy stopped at the end of the corridor and pushed against a white panelled door and went in. They followed her. She flicked at an ancient raised round Bakelite light switch with a single delicate pink nail-polished finger. Her hand was wide for her svelte body and long fingers.

A chandelier burst into life and glowed with bright white light from the high ceiling. The lights hung from an immense and elaborate ceiling rose. The room was humid and spacious. A large sash window rattled with the breeze outside. A gloomy yellow moon filtered through low grey clouds in a dark sky.

A king-sized bed sat back against one wall with a carved mahogany headboard. A dark-red duvet cover emblazoned with elaborate rose patterns lay puffed up on top. Matching pillows had wide feminine frills. Two massive Edwardian carved wardrobes stood side by side opposite the bed. Heavy purple flock-style wallpaper added to the oppressive ancient atmosphere. A more modern cream carpet provided the only light colour in the room.

David left the suitcases in the middle of the room and wiped his brow with the back of his hand. He threw himself onto the wide bed. Ruth dropped the holdall bags beside the suitcases.

"Madam Ruth and David," said Candy from the doorway. "You may freshen up in the bathroom next door. Lady Elena will receive you in her drawing-room in one hour. You should present yourselves to her in your uniforms. She'll expect you to wear them at all times when you are not in your room. David, your wardrobe is to the left and, Madam Ruth, yours is the other one. You are of similar sizes so I suppose it doesn't matter much which wardrobe you choose."

Candy curtsied to Ruth and left.

David whispered to his wife. "Why does she call you Madam Ruth? She's a weird one, she is."

Ruth shook her head and giggled. "What an odd woman. The curtsey, the strange clothes, how strange."

David said. "Why did she say it didn't matter what clothing we used? She's a strange woman. As if I'd wear female clothes, Ruth." They laughed.

David thought female clothes might not be such a bad idea, but in private not in front of his wife. He used to try Ruth's clothes on. But that wasn't real. It was that fantasy; great for masturbation sessions, nothing more. Not for sharing with your wife, that's for sure. It wasn't reality. Even so, the idea gave him warm feelings that zinged down to his penis.

Ruth showered first then David followed. He returned to the bedroom with a thick fluffy white towel wrapped around his waist. His short greying hair was plastered to his head, his small skinny body dripped. Ruth was already in her new uniform. She looked good in straight black trousers that finished a couple of inches above her ankles and a white blouse tucked in at the waist. She'd pulled her dark hair back tight into a long ponytail high on the back of her head.

"That's better," David said as he walked to the heavy old sash window and lifted it high to let in the cool night air. Air conditioning was a pointless dream in the ancient mansion.

The rain had stopped and the golden moon was rising higher through thinning clouds. An unseen animal, maybe a fox or a badger, disturbed a motion sensor the garden lit up from an unseen floodlight. A harsh white daylight glared. The first sight of the amount of lawn he'd be responsible for mowing filled him with concern. This would be no easy job. Nothing is.

His towel was whipped away and he stood naked. He turned to see Ruth running away, holding the towel up in her hand as if it were a prize. She was giggling. She may have been the most sensible of the two when it came to plans but she could be childish when relaxed. She appeared happy to be here with a job. Sometimes her sense of humour annoyed him. He laughed anyway and chased after her, catching her and trying to wrest the towel from her grip.

A light cough broke the moment. Candy was standing at the bedroom door. Her eyes, shadowed by large black false eyelashes and dusky eyeshadow, flitted down to David's penis. Her gaze remained on it for a few moments too long. David pulled his hands over it. He felt an unusual tingle in his stomach at his nakedness with two women. Candy had something attractive and he immediately felt guilty at his thoughts. A tingle flowed down causing a twitch in his penis. He willed it not to grow.

Candy's gaze fell back down to his groin area. He supposed she didn't get much opportunity to meet men, stuck out here in the countryside, working every day for Lady Elena. That had to be it. And he'd have to be careful, Ruth would not accept the slightest sign he found Candy attractive too.

The trouble was, he did.

Chapter 3 – Ready for Her Ladyship

"Lady Elena is expecting you in five minutes. I suggest you get dressed and follow me. She doesn't like to be kept waiting," Candy's voice warbled, her tone forced. Her eyes flowed over David again and he felt exposed.

"OK, Candy," answered David. "If you could turn round I'll get dressed now." Best not to show Ruth he was enjoying the situation a little more than he should.

Candy fixed her eyes on him. "Lady Elena's instructions were to ensure you're both attired correctly and for me to oversee this. It doesn't do to countermand Her Ladyship's instructions. I'll remain to make certain you are prepared as per her instructions, David."

His face flushed. "I do mind, Candy." He didn't but kept his hands clasped tight around his genitals.

Ruth's hand rested on David's arm. Her large round brown eyes slopped down in the corners with tiredness. "Candy, I don't like the idea of other women seeing my husband naked. It doesn't seem right."

Candy's face looked concerned for a moment. "Madam Ruth, David. It's only a penis, I've seen plenty in my time, especially in recent years. Anyway, I've seen yours too, David, so it now makes *little* difference."

David stiffened at her stress on *little*. Candy looked at David then down to his hands, a faint grin on her face, her eyebrows lifted a little.

His moment of anger subsided. Candy had something he couldn't put his finger on; she looked like a fantasy maid. That wasn't without its attractions. He had to block that from his mind, he was happily married to Ruth, a wonderful woman. Still, there's nothing wrong with fantasies, that's not being unfaithful.

"I don't know, Candy," said Ruth looking up at the ceiling. She was caught between not wanting to cause problems and her sense of right and wrong.

Candy shuffled on her heels, anxiety creased in her face and tears appeared in her eyes. "I'm sorry, Madam, but I've learnt not to disobey

Lady Elena's orders. If she says I have to ensure the correct attire and appearance, then that's what I must do. There will be repercussions if we don't do as she tells us."

Ruth laid her arm on David's shoulder then glared back at Candy. "I'm not happy, but, I don't know. I guess we can't disobey our new employer on the first day. I suppose it's only a penis. It doesn't seem right, but what's the harm I guess."

David kept quiet, the idea not unattractive to have Candy's eyes on his penis. It would be Ruth's decision.

"Please hurry, we don't have much time. Her Ladyship expects everything and everyone to be punctual." Candy was shifting on her feet as if standing on hot coals.

Lady Elena must be a bit of an ogre, thought David.

Ruth took both David's hands, moving them away from his penis. It was partially hard, a state Ruth spotted instantly with a furrowing of her eyebrows. "David, come on darling. Let's get on with it." Her gentle tone was not matched by her expression at seeing his partial hard-on.

Candy dipped a tiny curtsey to Ruth. "Thank you for your understanding, Madam Ruth."

He was sure Ruth would mention his erection later. She forgot nothing.

Ruth guided David by an arm to the wardrobe and she swung open the door. He kept one hand over his genitals. White shirts hung from on hangers and pairs of black trousers hanging below them. Two matching black jackets hung next to them.

The wardrobe had a set of drawers inside. A shoe rack sat beside them with two pairs of black flat shoes. David went to his suitcase and flicked it open with his free hand, keeping his back to Candy. He felt Candy's eyes on him. He shivered. Candy was attractive, in a tarty fetish sort of way. And she had those enormous breasts. Spilling. His mind filled with thoughts of his head nestled in them. He tightened his grip on his genitals. It wouldn't do to get an erection, things were already humiliating enough.

He rummaged through his case and found a pair of boxer shorts. He pulled them on and turned around, a small grin of triumph etched on his lips. He looked over to Ruth and she'd finished getting ready. She looked great, even in the uniform of flat-fronted slim-fit trousers and fitted white blouse. In her mid-forties, with that extra bit to cuddle, she was sexy. In a different way to Candy. Ruth's large oval brown eyes and chalk white skin the laugh lines radiating from the corners of her eyes. A wave of pride and love hit him.

David grabbed a shirt from the wardrobe, thankful his boxers hid his erection. He pulled it on. It didn't have any buttons. He poked at the front, unsure. There were buttonholes where the buttons should be and holes where buttons should be. He flicked through the other shirts. They were all the same.

"Candy, these are women's blouses," he said, his throat tight.

"Please hurry, David, Lady Elena does not like to be kept waiting."

David turned to face Candy, blouse hanging undone over striped boxers. "I can't wear women's blouses, where are my shirts?"

"This is your uniform. Lady Elena chose it herself. She would have her reasons, I wouldn't presume to ask her. Get dressed."

David stamped one foot. He grabbed a pair of trousers. There was no front zip. It was on the side. He searched through the other pairs. They were all identical.

"These are women's trousers," he said.

Candy breathed out a long sigh. "I must urge you to get dressed quickly, David. I have to remind you of Lady Elena's requirement for punctuality."

Ruth touched David's arm. "Darling, put them on and we'll speak with Lady Elena. I'm sure there's been some mistake. We can't afford to lose these jobs before we've even started. Besides, if you think about it, they're not a lot different from the male versions."

"Madam Ruth is correct, David. Please get dressed and follow me. Now. We have no time to lose."

David pulled the trousers on and zipped them up at the side. He looked down. They were two inches above his ankle. He did up the blouse with a show of reluctance and tucked it in. The trousers were tight and the outline of his boxer shorts showed clearly. He pushed his hands inside to attempt to smooth it down.

He fumed at his wife's practicality. He would discuss this with Lady Elena as soon as they met her and let her know in no uncertain terms this was not right.

Chapter 4 – Her Ladyship's rules

David and Ruth shuffled into the living room. David's courage deserted him.

Lady Elena Capel-Clifford sat upright in a large armchair, one slim leg crossed over the other. She looked even more impressive in the flesh than on a Zoom screen. Her long neck and back were as straight as a board. It was as if there was an invisible rod holding her body erect, even when sitting. Her forearms draped over each arm of the chair, long thin hands hung over each edge.

She held a paperback between two fingers. The cover was bright with the image of an attractive young lady and white bold writing on the front. It said it was a novel by an author called Lady Alexa. This must be one of her aristocratic friends. He saw the title, *A Sissy Cuckold Husband 1*. What a strange title. Lady Elena pushed the book down the side of the chair.

She wore a black cocktail dress as if dressed for a dinner party. Her silver hair lay loose onto smooth porcelain-white shoulders where it curled up in a single curl. Black dress straps were thin and bold against her shoulder skin. A pearl necklace hung around her long neck and into a deep cleavage that showed not a single wrinkle. Long silver earrings with pearls drops hung from small earlobes. They swung as she moved her head. Steely-blue eyes peered out from behind dusky grey eyeshadow.

Annabelle stood at her side, a hand on the back of the chair. Annabelle wore skin-tight riding trousers. She had a red jacket with black lapels, despite the heat, and black flat-heeled knee-high riding boots. She held a riding crop in her left hand; she tapped it against her thigh, beating out a frustrated rhythm.

David's eyes darted around the room, avoiding the two aristocrats' eye contact. He shuffled his hands clasped across his stomach. He glanced at Ruth who had a small smile on her lips. Her eyes sparkled. He guessed she was thinking about how they were safe now they had work and a place to live.

David wore flat-heeled shoes, black, plain and female. Why had Lady Elena wanted him in female clothing? This had to be a mistake, an oversight maybe.

He had put on a pair of his striped socks; the only other option had been the calf-high tan pantihose tights he had found in the wardrobe drawers. They had to be a mistake. The garish red and yellow socks peeked out from the gap between the bottom of his trouser legs and the shoes. Why were the trousers so short?

Candy had told him not to wear his socks; he'd ignored her suggestion. Ruth had shrugged and said it would be his problem. Lady Elena wouldn't be pleased, Candy had added. Really? What was she going to do?

Lady Elena looked him up and down. "D*aaaa*vid." She said stretching out the a. She shook her head and it swivelled as if on a ball-bearing base.

"I have provided you with perfectly acceptable pantihose tights to wear. So tell me. Daaaaavid, my dear. Why on Earth are you wearing those hideous socks?" My dear did not sound like an affectionate term.

David spluttered, she had no shame. She'd expected him to wear female clothing. Ruth poked him.

"With respect, Elena…," he began.

Lady Elena leant forward, menace drawn across her face. A slim manicured hand raised palm-out to him. "Goodness me," she said. Her eyes widened and she looked up at her daughter who raised her eyebrows and then back to David. She fixed him with a hard scowl. "It's *Lady*

Elena. Or Ma'am." She rested back on the chair. "You will never address me so informally ever again. Ever." She breathed out sharply from her nostrils and looked back at Annabelle. "Darling, I'm shocked. First names from the servants? What is the world coming to? It's all this equality and socialism that's to blame. There was a time everyone knew their place. The country's going to the dogs, I tell you. To the dogs."

Annabelle pursed her lips. "Try again, David."

Lady Elena's reaction knocked David's confidence, he looked to his wife who raised an eyebrow as if to say I told you so.

"Now, try again David. This time with the respect you should give to your betters. I'm a Lady you know, not one of your riff-raff working-class friends. Now. What is it you wish to tell me?"

He shuffled again, she was outmanoeuvring him and he was flustered. He glanced at Ruth who nodded at him to continue. "With respect. Ma'am." He shuffled again, head down, unused to calling anyone Ma'am. "The clothing you provided is female, I'd like to ask that you replace it with male clothing."

There he'd said it and his tightened shoulders dropped in relief. Now things would be settled.

Lady Elena's eyes rose to look at the ceiling, then back to him. "Your good wife has no problem with the uniform, I fail to understand why you do. I explained my uniform policy and you accepted this."

"Yes. Ma'am. But you didn't tell me it would be female clothing," he said, sensing things were not quite as resolved as he'd expected.

Lady Elena stood up. She smoothed her knee-length cocktail dress, the rings on her fingers glinted. "I fail to understand what that has to do with anything. This is the uniform, I expect my staff to wear identical uniforms; it's why it is called a *uniform*. If you do not wish to wear my free uniform then you may leave. I will find someone who will do as I require. There are plenty of people out of work at present. Do. I. Make. Myself. Clear?"

Ruth poked David in the ribs. She hissed at him. "Stop it, Davy. Say sorry to Lady Elena. We can't afford to mess this up."

Ruth's face was pinched, her eyes teary. He thought it best to follow his wife's advice and reflect on it later. He looked to the floor

"I'm sorry, Lady Elena."

His face flushed red. He wasn't accustomed to this type of humiliation. The trouble was his wife was correct, they couldn't afford to lose this job.

"Look up, Davy. There's a good boy." Lady Elena had picked up on Ruth's pet name for him.

He bridled at Lady Elena's use of Ruth's pet name. And the use of the word boy, what was that about? Lady Elena was an expert at being condescending and she was using her power. He raised his head as she'd asked and his gaze met the unblinking Lady Elena. From the corner of his eye, he saw Ruth looking at him in exasperation.

"Davy, Davy. What am I going to do with you?" It was clear Lady Elena wasn't going to drop his pet name. "Apologise to me correctly, boy. Look me in the eye and mean it. Tell me you will wear the attire I ask of you."

A grandfather clock in the corner of the room ticked like a time bomb. Annabelle's riding crop tapped against a riding boot in time to the clock.

David straightened up. "I'm sorry, Lady Elena. I'll wear what you expect me to wear next time."

Ruth breathed out in relief. A deep sigh escaped from Lady Elena's lips. She still wasn't happy about something.

"I understand this is new for you, Davy, but I expect your comportment to be as I desire. I want no discussion or debate with my servants. Goodness me. Your good wife is having no problems adapting to my rules." She sighed again. "I am willing to make an exception this one time as you're new. However, I do not want you to get it right *next time.* I want you correctly attired *this time.*" She shook her head and her hair moved as one block.

She got up and strode towards him, like a model on a catwalk, one foot in line with the other. She was tall and erect with an air of menace. The idea of her as a lioness on the hunt came to his mind. She walked around him and Ruth and back to stand in front of him. She was much taller than David in her heels. She ran a hand over his hip and down his bottom. He flinched, what was she doing now?

"Davy, Davy. I suspect you're going to take some work." She said nothing more, staring down at him, eye to eye.

He waited, but she said nothing more. Ruth dug a finger into his side. "Say, yes, Lady Elena," she whispered.

Lady Elena moved in closer, two inches from his face. Her rich fruity perfume washed around him. "What, may I enquire, are you wearing beneath your trousers. Boy?"

His forehead creased. "Boxer shorts, Ma'am. Why?"

"Boxer shorts," she stated, moving away. "Boxer shorts." She shook her head.

David tried to step away too but Ruth's palm rested on his back.

"Boxer shorts spoil the line of fitted trousers. I will not have my staff dressed like untidy tramps. I have provided several sets of acceptable underwear, as well as pantihose tights. Return upstairs and change into the correct attire. Then return here." She moved away and returned to her seat. "Now would be appropriate, my dear boy." She waved a hand dismissively.

David scuttled away and ran up the stairs, taking two at a time, to the bedroom. He pulled open the wardrobe drawers. They were stuffed with cotton female panties in pinks, whites and yellows. All had a small bow at the front. He had no time to think about it. He removed his trousers, socks and boxers. He put on a pair of white panties and pulled on the calf-high pantihose tights. A slight squeal of the floorboards came from behind. He spun around. Candy was standing in the doorway.

"That's much better, Davy. If you'd have listened to me, you would have avoided this little episode. Lady Elena is a stickler for her rules. Now put your clothes on and come back downstairs so Her Ladyship may inspect you. I'm afraid you haven't made a very good first impression. You only remain in employment because Lady Elena is impressed by your Mistress, Madam Ruth. However, this won't last much longer if you continue to rebel." Candy's eyes flicked do to the front of his panties, bulging like a package with his penis and balls.

What was Candy talking about, *his Mistress*? David didn't have time to think about that and pulled on his trousers. He followed Candy back down the stairs to Lady Elena. What had he got himself into? Things couldn't get any more humiliating, that much was sure.

Chapter 5 - A Housemaid's Role

David did not want a repeat of his humiliation with Lady Elena two days ago. He focussed on doing exactly as she said. Ruth reminded him the job was not going to work out if he disobeyed Lady Elena's rules, however odd they seemed. He wore the uniform she provided, along with the female panties and tights and flat female shoes.

Lady Elena assigned him as her butler with Candy assigned to cleaning and other housework. They didn't cross paths for two days. He helped Ruth to cook. Lady Elena preferred Ruth to cook and for him to serve dinner at the table or to serve coffee and tea. She had a little bell she tinkled when she wanted him. Late morning and the bell tinkled from the front room.

He went in. "Yes, Lady Elena."

Heavy purple curtains were drawn back and light poured in. Outside, a large silver limousine pulled up, the tyres crunching on the gravel driveway.

"Sir Rupert Jones has come to visit. He's our local Member of Parliament. He's popping in for tea, a piece of cake and some light relief. Please let him in and show him here, Davy."

"Yes, Ma'am." David wasn't going to make the mistakes of a couple of days ago. He'd suffered the wrath of Ruth for not complying with Lady Elena's instructions. She had also made her feelings clear about his erection with

Candy. He'd managed to placate her by assuring her it was his attraction to her and not to the over made-up bimbo of a housemaid. She accepted his lie.

David went to the front door and opened it. A tall overweight man with a red nose and broken veins on his cheeks panted onto the top step.

"I'll never know why Lady Elena doesn't get a stairlift installed." He looked up at David. "Who the hell are you? Where's Candy?"

"I don't know," David said, then remembered Ruth's instructions to be respectful. "Sir Rupert."

Sir Rupert huffed and puffed and barged in. His face was red and he wiped the sweat from his face with a handkerchief

"This way, Sir, Lady Elena is waiting for you." David led him to the front room.

Sir Rupert humpfed. "Where the devil is that little scamp Candy? A pair of bongos like the Welsh mountains. Handsome woman." He held out his hands as if grasping a pair of breasts.

Handsome wasn't how David would have described Candy, although he wouldn't disagree with Sir Rupert's analogy for her breasts. They walked into the front room and Sir Rupert and Lady Elena greeted each other with air kisses.

Lady Elena turned to Davy. "Bring tea, scones and two slices of raspberry cake and put them in the dining room, Davy."

Sir Rupert huffed. "Who's this Davy fellow? What have you done with that lovely bint Candy? What's going on here, Elena?"

"Nothing, Rupy dear. I've taken on a couple more employees to help Candy out."

"Humpf," said Sir Rupert. "I don't want Davy-boy replacing Candy."

Lady Elena guided Sir Rupert to a chair. "Don't worry Rupy, he won't be."

David left the room, catching Sir Rupert's *humpf* reply, and went to the kitchen.

Ruth was cutting and peeling, preparing food for dinner. He made tea, filling the china teapot with hot water, putting two bone china cups and saucers onto a silver tray. He put a bowl of sugar cubes on the tray, two slices of cake and two scones on matching plates and a little milk in a small jug. He walked out to the hall.

The dining room door was open and he went in to place the tray on the dining table as Lady Elena had asked. There was no one there. He heard muffled voices from the front room. They were still there. He'd take the tea to them there. Initiative. Lady Elena would be pleased.

He left the dining room and went to the hall. As he approached the door, he heard lady Elena speaking. "Good girl, slow, gentle. How Sir Rupert likes it."

He pushed into the room. Lady Elena was seated, sat back legs crossed. Sir Rupert was standing a couple of feet away from her, his back to David, trousers around his ankles. A large fat bum faced David and two pairs of glaring shocked eyes.

Lady Elena stood. "Get out. I told you to serve it in the dining room."

David froze a moment. A huge mop of blond hair moved out from behind Sir Rupert at groin level. Candy. Sir Rupert turned. His huge erect penis, firm and red, pointed at David. David staggered back, grasping at his tray.

Lady Elena looked down at Candy. "Don't stop, stupid girl." She pointed at Davy. "I said out."

David back out of the door as he saw Candy's mouth move over Sir Rupert's enormous hard cock to the end. David shot out to the dining room, dropped the tray on the dining room and fled to the kitchen.

There was something very odd going on in this house.

Chapter 6 – Show Respect

Lady Elena never mentioned his walking in on Candy giving Sir Rupert a blow job in the front room. She told him later to ensure he followed her instructions exactly and to not use his initiative. Ruth told him that the wealthy were not like them and they thought the normal rules didn't apply to them. That was looking true.

He became accustomed to the female clothing over the week, they were not that female. At least it wasn't a skirt. He didn't like it but, as Ruth pointed out many times over the week, they were plain. All in black or white. It was nothing to lose a job over, especially a job so important to their survival.

Five days after the blow-job incident, David was serving evening dinner to Lady Elena in the dining room. Lady Elena sat at the head of the table and Annabelle to her right. He placed the dinner plates in front of the two ladies, poured them a glass of wine, and went to return to the kitchen to eat with his wife.

"It's time for the next stage, *mater*," Annabelle spoke out sharply while staring at him. "I can't abide this much longer."

Annabelle's use of the Latin word *mater* for *mother* struck him as affected. He continued towards the kitchen doors, keen to get away and back to his wife where he could relax. He assumed Annabelle was referring to something that had little to do with him. Yet, she had looked directly at him.

"Yes of course. You're quite correct, Annabelle. Thank you for the reminder," Lady Elena said and also looked at him.

He pushed against the kitchen.

"Davy, would you kindly ask your good wife to come here with you? Now."

He stopped, a hand on the door. Lady Elena often used expressions like *kindly* or *if you would be so kind* when she was being anything but kind.

"Yes, Madam." He pushed against the door and went into the kitchen.

He told Ruth Lady Elena wanted to see them both immediately. She wiped her hands on her apron, removed it from around her waist and shrugged her shoulders. They went into the dining room. Lady Elena pointed to a spot a couple of feet to the side of her. She swung her long elegant legs round to face them. David and Ruth stopped in the indicated spot, side by side, their hands behind their backs.

"Ruth, Davy." She looked to them one at a time. There was no expression on her wrinkle-free face, her skin like fine china, her blue eyes sparkled. "You've done well this past week. I understand you've never been in service before so this is all new for you. Because of this, I've been lenient, particularly with respect to the correct etiquette around the home. And Davy's little error the other day with Sir Rupert." She chuckled.

David and Ruth exchanged glances, struggling to not smile at the memory.

Lady Elena continued. "I am content with you both and things are working out."

Smiles grew across their faces. "Thank you, Madam," they said together.

Annabelle fidgeted and slid back her chair. "*Mater*. Get on with it," her voice petulant.

An indulgent smile spread across Lady Elena's face. "The young. So impatient."

Annabelle looked to the ceiling.

"So, back to the reason I called you both here." She looked from David to Ruth. "I want to speak about the next stage in your domestic duties. I insist on my domestic workers showing me, and my daughter, the correct level of respect."

Annabelle looked back up to the ceiling.

Lady Elena continued. "Respect means addressing me, and Annabelle, as Ma'am or Lady Elena. But I also expect a demonstration of respect when you enter or leave the room and when taking my instructions. Do you understand what I am talking about?"

David and Ruth looked at each other. David had no idea what she was on about. "No Madam, I'm afraid I don't understand." He looked back at Ruth. "Do you, dear?"

Ruth shook her head. Her lips pursed.

Lady Elena waved her hand airily. "Of course, of course, silly me. You won't understand, you have never been in domestic service before. Especially for someone as well-bred as I am." She sat up. "What I mean to say is, as my domestic staff, you will curtsey to me when leaving or entering the room and when taking orders."

David's mouth dropped open.

"Mater?" Annabelle barked.

"Oh yes," Lady Elena replied, the indulgent smile returning. "You will curtsey to Annabelle too, naturally."

David went to speak but Ruth poked him in the ribs. He pulled on his reserves of control. He cleared his throat, he needed to correct her.

"Yes, Madam, I understand. Of course I do. But don't you mean for me to bow a little, drop my head in respect? That's fine. I understand." He puffed himself up, pleased he hadn't caused another problem.

Lady Elena raised her eyebrows and Annabelle puffed her cheeks. "No Davy, I know exactly what I mean. I don't require your correction. You will *curtsey* to us."

David's shoulders drooped. There must be some mistake. "But, Ma'am. Women curtsey, men bow. I'm happy to bow my head. It will be no problem."

A flush of red bloomed through Lady Elena's cheeks. "Do not contradict me, Davy, I said I know exactly what I want to say. You will curtsey. I do not want you bowing like some stage performer. No. You are my domestic employees and you will show the correct respectful response." Her hands went to her lap. "You can reply with a '*Yes, Ma'am,*' and curtsey. Knees bent, one leg back and hold your hands out as if holding an imaginary dress. We will begin this from now on."

"Yes, Ma'am," Ruth replied, head down. She performed a perfect curtsey. Lady Elena glared at David. Her eyes narrowed. "And your curtsey, Davy?"

David looked down at his feet.

"Do it, Davy, or else." Ruth stage whispered

"Or else what?" He glared at her.

A cough broke their argument. "When you two have quite finished your little domestic spat, I'm waiting to see Davy curtsey."

David cringed at Lady Elena calling him Davy. It was reserved for Ruth. Something intimate, close. Ruth didn't seem to have noticed but gave him another dig to the ribs. Her slitted eyes told he was going to have to curtsey and she was not going to help him get out of it.

All eyes were on David; he felt his heart thumping. Heat rose from his neck to the top of his head. He dipped quickly and waved his arms out and back. He hoped it would be enough. He knew it wasn't.

Chapter 7 – The Training Session

"No, no, no, Davy," sighed Lady Elena. She turned to her daughter. "Annabelle dear, would you spend some time training Davy?"

Annabelle's face broke into a wide grin. "It would be my pleasure, mater. *Yah.*"

Lady Elena sighed long and deep. "Ruth dear, you may return to the kitchen. Leave your errant husband with Annabelle. She will teach him how to behave. He will be in good hands and learn. They all do, they enjoy it."

David looked back at Lady Elena– *they enjoy it?*

Ruth dipped a formal curtsey. "Yes, Madam, of course. We'll both be happy to do this." She poked David in the chest. "And you will do exactly as Madam Annabelle tells you. Do you understand me, Davy?"

David gasped at his wife's sharp anger. He nodded. She returned to the kitchen.

Lady Elena pushed her dinner plate away and left the room by the hallway door. Annabelle strode over to David and circled him. She wore her usual tight riding breeches which outlined her strong legs and ample rounded bottom. She wore knee-high black riding boots, despite being indoors. She walked over to the side of the room and retrieved a riding crop. She walked back with long strides, tapping her boots as she went.

Thwack. She slapped her crop hard against one boot. "Curtsey, Davy. Now." She circled behind him.

He dipped down as Ruth had done. Then stood straight. Pressure built in his head. This was beyond humiliation.

"Not bad, Davy. But this time, hold your hands out from your body. As if holding out a pretty dress. Imagine that fine material in your fingers. That would be nice, *yah*? Wearing a pretty dress? You'd like that?"

She tapped him lightly on the bottom three times with the crop as his blood pressure rose at her taunts. He jumped a little, from the surprise. He dipped down again in a simile of a curtsey, this time holding his hands out as she had instructed. Like a ballet dancer. How could Ruth accept this?

"Excellent, Daisy. Now again." Her voice taunting with a little excitement around the edge.

Did he hear what he thought he'd heard? "Excuse me, Madam, my name is David."

Annabelle looked perplexed for a minute. "*Yah* of course, what did I say?"

"You called me Daisy, Madam."

Annabelle put a hand to her mouth and giggled. "Did I? Silly me."

He wasn't sure now whether she was teasing him or had mispronounced his name. "Yes, Madam."

"Anyway, *yah*, whatever. Daisy, Davy, Danni, Debbie, Daphne. Another curtsey, if you please. Debbie." She laughed loudly at her own joke.

He repeated the curtsey, a look of satisfaction spread across her face. She walked back and forth across him, still tapping her boot with the riding crop. She tapped his bottom again. "And again, Delia." She giggled, getting into her joke.

He curtsied. Arms out like a ballerina.

Annabelle squealed in delight. "Excellent. *Yah*, I believe you've got it." She stopped pacing. "You can go now and help your good wife in the kitchen."

Annabelle was annoying him. This young woman thought she was superior to him because she was the daughter of an aristocrat. He turned towards the kitchen but stopped at the sound of Annabelle clearing her throat.

"Haven't you forgotten something?"

He swallowed hard. She expected a curtsey. This was going to be a tougher job than he had expected. He swung round to face her. He curtsied low and held out his hands.

She waved her crop towards the kitchen door. "OK, off you go, Well done, Daisy."

The name *Daisy* dug into his ears like the point of a knife blade. "Excuse me, Madam, it's Davy or David." He wanted some victory from now having to curtsey like a housemaid in Victorian times. Even getting her to call him by his proper name would count as something. There was no victory coming.

"*Yah,* whatever." She tapped the crop on her thigh once. "*Dolly.*"

Chapter 8 - New Job New Clothes

"I wish you wouldn't keep on moaning about Annabelle calling you Daisy or Debbie and having to curtsey." Ruth was washing up the breakfast plates. "You know what Lady Elena and her daughter are like. They are absent-minded, a little thoughtless. But that's all; aristocrats are like that, they don't mean anything by it, they live in a different world. Let it go, Davy."

David dried the dishes by hand, his cloth soaked by the number of dishes he had to dry. He wondered why someone as wealthy as Lady Elena couldn't buy a dishwasher machine. He supposed she didn't even think about it; it wasn't as if she did the dishes. He stared out of the kitchen window across the paved patio. Large potted plants looked like they needed some care and attention. The huge lawn needed a cut. He guessed he'd be asked to do that very soon.

The sky was a cloudless blue, the sun throwing a long shadow from the tall house across the lawn. The forecast was for a mini-heatwave: 30C/86F. On the plus side, he could take off his shirt and get some colour in the sun while mowing.

He didn't understand why Ruth was being so relaxed about him having to wear female clothing and with Annabelle calling him Daisy. Yes, the clothes were trousers and blouses and yes, they were plain. At a distance, they could be mistaken for being unisex. But he knew they were female. Ruth was more worried about the job than his feelings and Annabelle's teasing. That wasn't like her, she was usually so caring.

On the plus side, his new clothes were softer and made from finer material than male clothing; so much better for the forecasted heat of the next week. 30C today and 35C/95F by the end of the week, according to BBC Radio4 news. The BBC was the only network Lady Elena would allow on in the house. The commercial stations were not British enough, she was fond of saying. They sounded fine to him but it wasn't his house.

Now he had to put up with this curtseying nonsense. He could have understood having to bow, maybe. But a curtsey? A female movement? Ruth had brushed his complaints away, telling him not to be so sensitive. Lady Elena had explained her issues with bowing, Ruth said. She thought it was something a stage performer did. If that was her opinion then so be it, she said. Practical Ruth. *So be it,* another of her fallback catchphrases. He ground his teeth at the thought.

Ruth wasn't concerned when he'd told her Annabelle had 'accidentally' called him Daisy and Daphne and Debbie. There was something mischievous in Annabelle's eyes. His wife was uninterested. She told him last night to ignore them when they made these little mistakes. The trouble was their 'little' mistakes were always with him. It was him who had to wear female trousers, him who had to curtsey like a housemaid. And him Annabelle called Daisy. And Daphne. And Debbie.

Annabelle burst into the kitchen, riding boots squeaking on the tiled floor. "Ruth, Daisy," she called out breathlessly.

David placed the drying up cloth on the drainer. "It's Davy, Madam."

Annabelle waved a hand in the air. "*Yah, whatever.*"

David looked at his wife whose eyes went to the ceiling. She aimed a glare at him.

"Mater wants you to work on the garden today. It's become so untidy since the gardener left and Candy can do the housework and cooking." Annabelle seemed to think about something distasteful for a moment and her nose crinkled. "Manual work is so working class, don't you think?" It wasn't a question. "Finish what you are doing then meet me outside. I'll show you where the garden implement *thingies* are stored and where we keep the sit-on mower. I will provide work clothes and boots for you both. It won't do to get these nice smart indoor clothes all dirty and sweaty, would it? Besides, you'll be wanting something lighter and cooler in this heat."

Ruth dipped a curtsey and replied, "Yes Madam. Thank you, Madam"

David frowned. He didn't like his wife's newfound obsequiousness when Lady Elena and Annabelle were around. What had happened to the proud independent Ruth he used to know. He knew it was for the job but she had slipped into it too easily. It was as if she were over-awed by being around aristocracy.

"Thank you, Madam," he said in a flat tone, then curtsied too. His frown deepened.

A thin smile flitted across Annabelle's face. She spun on her boot heels and left through the back door, leaving it ajar.

David and Ruth dried their hands and followed her a few seconds later. Outside, Annabelle pointed to a large wooden shed. "The garden tools are stored in there. At the back, you'll find the sit-on mower."

She picked up two pairs of black training-style shoes as if they were made of dog poop. They didn't look too bad, thought David.

She pointed to a large cardboard box under the kitchen window. It was still taped up with the address labels on the top. "Your summer gardening clothes are in the box. They're your gardening uniform. You'll find green tee shirts, that sort of thing. You're both the same size so everything will fit either of you."

David looked at her.

"The box won't open itself, *Debbie*." Annabelle folded her arms under her large bosom.

David glowered at Ruth who shook her head and raised a finger to him. A side smirk grew across Annabelle's lips.

David knelt by the box and ripped the brown plastic tape from the top, lifted the flaps and peered inside. Several brand-new tee-shirts were folded inside clear plastic covers. He rummaged through the pile. There were several pairs of shorts in the same shade of green in the next pile, tightly folded into sharp folds. He pulled out a tee shirt and a pair of shorts, passed them to Ruth, and pulled two packets out for himself.

"Put your gardening clothes on and I'll show you what I want you to do." Annabelle smiled.

David ripped off the plastic from the tee shirt and held it out. It was a dark green tennis-style shirt in the material they use for sports tops. This will be nice and cool for working in the garden in the heat. This was better.

He glanced up at Annabelle. "I'll go inside and slip my clothes on, Madam."

Annabelle moved across the door back to the kitchen. "There is no one around, *Diana,* and we are miles from anywhere. You can get changed here on the patio. *Yah.*"

"But..."

Ruth dug him in the ribs. It was becoming her method of shutting him up. "Put the work clothes on, Davy, I'm sure Madam Annabelle is not bothered about seeing you in your underwear. It's easier and quicker to get changed here rather than all the fuss of going indoors, getting changed and then coming back out." She breathed out in exasperation, looked at Annabelle, and shook her head.

Annabelle nodded, her face serious, her eyes sparkling with mischief. "Quite correct Ruth. Come on *Denise*, I don't have all day."

Girl's names, all beginning with D, she was taking the piss. She was goading him, testing him. Ruth pulled off her blouse and stepped out of her trousers. She stood in her underwear. "See, Davy. It's not so difficult." She pulled the green tennis shirt over her head, tugged it down and stared at him.

He supposed there was some truth in what Ruth had said. Annabelle wouldn't be interested in seeing his scrawny little body. It was probably easier and quicker. All the same, the was something wrong about him having to stand in a pair of women's panties. He had to get on with it, whatever his feelings. He wasn't going to find any support from Ruth, she had got completely into the servile lifestyle.

He stripped down to his panties, folded his blouse and trousers, placed them on a small table. He pulled on the tee shirt. It was light and airy. Not bad.

He saw Ruth pull on her shorts from the corner of his eye. She pulled them up and adjusted them around her waist, tugging on the elastic waistband until she was comfortable. They were short. And not shorts. It was a pencil-pleated tennis skirt, in the same light sports material as the top. He admired his wife's legs, she looked good for her age. She twirled back and forth, grinning as the little skirt swirled around her legs.

Annabelle clapped twice and broke his thoughts. "Come on *Daisy*, get your things on. I have horse-jumping practice over in the village paddocks in a bit. I don't have all day to waste sorting out the servants."

He ripped open the packet with the shorts in and held them out. It was a mini tennis skirt too. "Whoops," he said. "I must have picked out two skirts."

David knelt back by the box and rifled through the pile. He flicked through to the bottom and looked up at Annabelle. "They are *all* little skirts."

Annabelle raised her eyebrows. "That's very observant of you, *Daniella*." A smile came over her lips that didn't reach her eyes. "And that should be, they are all little skirts, *Ma'am*."

Chapter 9 - The Pretty Tennis Skirt

"So where are the shorts for me?" He swallowed hard. "Ma'am."

"Better, Daisy. And there aren't any shorts. It was easier to get all the same things. So I did. No shorts. Just skirts." Annabelle's put a thumb and forefinger to her face and put her head to one side in fake concern. "Sorry about that. Didn't think." Her eyes glinted.

"Excuse me?" He looked back into the box. "Ma'am."

"Why should I excuse you, *Demi*?" said Annabelle. "Are you hard of hearing? Did you not listen to me? Do you not understand English?

Donna, I expect much better from my servants. You still have much to learn."

Ruth leant over him and touched his shoulder. "Davy, please."

He brushed her hand away and stood. He put his hands hard on his hips, digging his fingers hard into his stomach. He opened his mouth to speak, rage flowed through and around him. It was as if his face was about to explode.

"Davy, don't." Ruth's voice was firm and deep. Something in her tone held him back.

"No, *Daisy*, don't." Annabelle's voice had a barely constrained laugh floating in it.

David took a long deep breath. Was this humiliation worth it? He looked into Ruth's eyes; they pleaded. "Please don't muck this up," she said. Her voice was a low whisper. Her tone struck something in him. He hesitated.

"No, *Daisy*, do not muck this up or your little servant job will be flowing away down that river at the bottom of the garden." She pointed a thumb over her shoulder.

He turned to Ruth. "What should I do?"

Ruth looked away an instant and back. "Davy, you're going to have to put the skirt on."

He stepped back. "You can't be serious?"

Annabelle moved to him. "*Daisy*." Her tone changed, there was a hard threat in it. "Put the damn skirt on and get to work." She huffed loudly. "Good grief. Mater wants the grass cut, not a debate about pretty skirts with the servants. I'm now late for horse riding." She pushed her face into his. "Put the damn skirt on and get to work." Her voice raised a level, shrill and angry.

Ruth nodded at him. He was cornered. He took the skirt packet out and tore off the plastic. Ruth flipped open the top button of his trousers, pulled down the zipper and they fell to his ankles. He stepped out of them, conscious of being in little female panties. Annabelle's fell to his bulge at the front. Another smile flitted across her face.

"Not much down there to worry about, Daisy. Small and feminine." Annabelle's tone was mocking.

Ruth shook her head at him. He stepped into the skirt and pulled it to his waist. Ruth smiled a little and fought not to laugh. One of Annabelle's eyebrows raised. "That wasn't so hard was it, Daisy-poppet?"

David looked down at the little skirt, his skinny legs hairy below the short hem.

Ruth put her head into his. "You look lovely, dear."

Annabelle looked him up and down. "*Yah*, Daisy-Missy, you look very pretty princess."

David wanted the two women to stop looking at him. Or did he? The worst of it was their looks were admiring. Annabelle had to be mad, but Ruth looked comfortable with him in a skirt. He wasn't going to tell anyone the feeling of the light breeze around his legs and up the short skirt and round his balls was not unpleasant. Especially with Annabelle's mocking. He liked that. He hated himself for liking it.

Ruth looked him up and down, a kind smile across her face. "Davy, be practical. It's hot and a little skirt will be much cooler for working in than shorts. And there's no one else to see you if wearing a skirt hurts your male pride. Anyway, who said men can't wear skirts?"

Ruth, ever the practical one. He put his hands to the skirt. It was light and soft. The pleats were sharp and tight. It felt good, like Ruth's skirts he'd tried on when she was out. This time Ruth was with him. And she didn't mind that at all. She liked it. So did he.

"Well, well. I didn't expect that."

He spun around, his hands still pressed against his little skirt. Lady Elena stood in the back doorway.

"Very pretty, Davy. Or should I call you Daisy, as my daughter does? I see you wanted to wear something more practical for this heat. Well done. I have to say I am pleased with your attitude in recent days. But a skirt is a development I am very pleased with."

Her eyes flowed over him and he blushed.

"I did not expect this quite so soon. I thought it may take a little longer to get you there. Better earlier than later. We don't like masculinity polluting our daily life here, not that you ever threatened to be manly. Anyway, better this than you presenting as a man, however unmanly you are." She nodded to herself, looking at his legs. "You need a little more work. Another time, first get to work."

David was speechless. What was she talking about, they had wanted him in a skirt? Whatever for? Ruth smiled at Lady Elena who bent down and picked up a small cardboard box next to the large box he'd unpacked. David hadn't noticed it.

"I guess you won't be needing these now." Lady Elena held the small box to her chest.

"Need what, Ma'am?" David said.

Lady Elena's eyes flicked to her daughter and back to David. Questions flowing into her sharp mind. "The work shorts. In this box, Daisy." She looked again at her daughter.

David gasped. Annabelle had tricked him. "But Madam, I didn't see the other box. Madam Annabelle only gave me the option to wear a skirt."

Lady Elena looked at Annabelle. "Is this true, Darling? You made him put on a skirt? Tut, tut. Naughty daughter."

Annabelle glared at David. "I never forced him to do anything. He put the skirt on with no pressure from me. Isn't it true Ruth?"

Ruth's mouth opened and shut. David could see she wasn't sure how to respond. "Well," Ruth started. "I suppose Davy did put it on voluntarily and without complaint." She looked at her feet.

Lady Elena moved up to him and ran a hand down his little skirt and to his bare thigh. "I expect this feels wonderful, Daisy?"

He was distraught to feel his penis growing hard. He had been fighting it. Now he'd lost the fight and it reacted strongly. The attention and comments he was getting made the situation worse. He opened his mouth to reply, his tongue on the point of forming 'no' in reply to Lady Elena's question. A dig in his ribs stopped him. Ruth's glare and a mouthed '*don't*' told him how he had to reply.

"Yes, Madam," he said, his eyes down on the floor. "Thank you."

"Lady Elena is expecting a curtsey, Davy." Ruth dug his ribs again.

He dipped a small curtsey, holding out the ends of his little pleated tennis skirt.

"Excellent, excellent." Lady Elena's eyes ran up and down David's legs and skirt. "Annabelle, can you ask Candy to lay out their new summer outfits for serving dinner tonight? It is time for the next stage. This is all proceeding much quicker than I expected. He's an easy one."

She faced David and ran a hand up his thigh and up to his bottom. What did that mean, he thought. *An easy one?*

"Annabelle, would you kindly ask Candy to help Daisy look the part? His legs are most untidy. I imagine other parts too." Lady Elena said. She looked at him again in thought. "Her. Yes time to use her."

David's eyes widened. What summer outfits? What was she on about? Her?

Ruth took his hand. "Come on Davy, let's get to work."

"Oh no, Ruth," Annabelle said. "Now she's in a pretty skirt you should call her Daisy."

David and Ruth stopped. They looked into each other's eyes. Ruth opened her mouth, looked at Annabelle, and back to David. She closed her mouth and opened it again as if the words she wanted would come. She swallowed. "Come on, Let's get to work."

She looked to Annabelle and Lady Elena. She looked back at David. "Daisy."

Chapter 10 – The Housemaid Came

Ruth lay her hand on David's bare thigh, caressing his skin and playing with his leg hairs. Her fingers slid under the hem of the little tennis skirt and up the erection that poked up inside his panties. She touched the end of his erection with a fingertip. It was damp.

Amusement danced in Ruth's face. It had been some time since they had made love. The feel of the light skirt on his thighs and his wife's fingers near to his penis made him feel desperate.

They lay on their bed, the sun beaming through the window. Dust motes shimmered in the light. Outside the window, a swarm of tiny midges danced in random patterns. His legs and back ached from the day working in the garden. He was sticky and sweaty and wanted a shower.

He asked her why she hadn't stuck up for him more when Lady Elena and Annabelle humiliating him.

"I don't know, Davy. I'm a little conflicted myself. I don't think they mean to embarrass you, they believe they are helping." She sat up. "Or should I be calling you Daisy too?" She grinned.

David pushed her arm in a friendly manner. He was too tired and fed up to fight.

"Please don't tease me, Ruth. I want to know how I got into this situation and why you went along with it."

Ruth pressed her hand onto his penis beneath the skirt. "It doesn't seem you're *that* upset about it if this is anything to go by." She squeezed his erection through his panties. "And besides, I notice you haven't removed your little skirt yet."

He sat up and thought for a short moment. She had a point; why hadn't he removed it. He hated it, didn't he? Spending the day working in the little skirt had made him feel heady and horny for some reason. The truth was he hadn't wanted to remove it and he had pretended he was too tired. He put on a serious face. He couldn't admit this to his wife.

"Ruth, don't tease." His comment came out weakly.

There was a light tap at the door and, before they could continue their discussion, Candy came in. She wore a black maid's dress with a small white frilly white apron tied around the front. She had two side ponytails, tied from the centre of each temple, held with two large pink ribbons. She wore black fishnet stockings and her shoes were black patent leather with steep heels. They glimpsed large white satin panties under the short dress.

"Lady Elena has asked me to help Daisy get prepared for this evening. She has guests and she wants her to look her best for serving at dinner. Ruth, you'll be working in the kitchen, I've hung up your new uniform dress for tonight. I have a new uniform for Daisy too."

David slid off the end of the bed, holding down his skirt. "My name is David," he snapped.

"Don't pick on Candy, Davy. She's only doing what Lady Elena and Annabelle tell her. It's not her fault.

David glared at his wife. "Yes, I know, but I don't like them calling me Daisy. It's humiliating."

"You're going to have to get used to it if that's what they want to call you. Can I remind you we have little choice? Besides, it's kind of cute. Daisy suits you. Especially in the cute little skirt."

David's face went red with anger, a stabbing pain shot into his forehead.

Candy spoke. "Please. Daisy. I need to get you ready, please come with me to the bathroom and get ready or we'll both be in trouble."

David let out a deep long sigh. He was still turned on from Ruth's hand on his leg and erect penis and, from wearing the panties and skirt. There was no time to try to go any further with his wife now, Candy was standing there being insistent. He was hot though.

"OK, I'm coming, Candy." he slid off the bed reluctantly.

Candy replied to Ruth. "I'll look after him while you get ready, Ruth." Ruth nodded at her, a sudden look of concern flashed across her face.

He followed Candy out of the room and into the bathroom next door. She was slim, bordering on skinny. . Her movements were girly-girl. Too much. She was pretty for an older woman, albeit too heavily made-up. There was something not right about Candy. He couldn't put his finger on what it was. Something in her face wasn't right, something in her movements seemed too affected. It was as if she had been trained and it wasn't entirely natural.

They entered the bathroom which C had already prepared. It was full of steam and the bath full of bubbles.

"Lady Elena asked that you have a bath so I can help you prepare for this evening."

"I don't need any help, thank you Candy." The idea he might like some help flashed through his mind. He pushed it away. The picture of Candy giving Sir Rupert a blow job came to him.

Candy's eyes flitted down to David's skirt then back up. Her eyes widened for a moment.

David's erection had not gone down and a tell-tale bulge was pushing out the front of his skirt.

Candy's mouth pursed. "Lady Elena said I'm to stay here with you to make sure you're prepared."

David let out another sigh. "You mean you're going to stay here while I undress and have a bath?"

"Yes, daisy."

David ran his hands through his short hair. "Please don't call me Daisy." He added. "Yes, yes, I know. Lady Elena told you to call me Daisy."

David's eyes fell on Candy's low-cut front. *Nice tits.* Completely over-the-top for her slim body size, but firm for a woman her age. He felt a deep discomfort go through him remembering Ruth was in the next room. She had seemed unconcerned about them being together in the bathroom. He guessed she wouldn't be so keen if she knew Candy would be watching him have a bath.

He called out. "Ruth, Candy says she has to stay here while I undress and bathe. Why don't you come here instead."

Ruth popped her head around the corner. "I'm going downstairs to shower and get ready and start dinner. Do whatever Candy tells you. We had this discussion earlier. It's not ideal, but there it is. Lady Elena's order."

"But Candy will see me naked," he whined.

"David, I've got to go."

Ruth shot away and her footsteps disappeared down the hallway. He turned back to Candy. She put her head on one side and her eyes widened.

"Shall we get undressed, Daisy?"

David snorted. "Please don't call me that name, Candy."

"Lady Elena's orders."

David knew it was useless. Ruth was right. He'd have to put up with it. Daisy it was. Another rung climbed on the ladder towards humiliation. First. He had to bathe in front of this bimbo.

Chapter 11 – Foam Bath & Bubbles

"Clothes off and jump in the bath, Daisy." Candy's open palm indicated the full bath with crackling bubbles.

"Could you turn around?"

"I could Daisy, but I'm going to be seeing you naked anyway so you may as well undress with me watching."

David was beaten again. Maybe it wouldn't be so bad. Candy was an exaggerated bimbo of a maid although there was something faintly masculine about her. He supposed that was her height. There was nothing masculine about her breast cleavage and long smooth legs.

David pulled off his tee-shirt and stood in his little pleated skirt. His erection was stubborn and strong. He'd been hard on and off for much of the day. Every time he felt the wind around his balls and thighs, every time his skirt had flailed in the breeze. After the teasing from his wife, his penis had remained stiff. He pulled down his skirt and stepped out of it. His erection strained against his small panties.

"Come on Daisy, you can't have a bath in your panties. Off." She indicated a lowering of his panties, her eyes fixed on his erection bulge.

David slid his finger in the small elasticated waistband. He pulled them down to the top of his erection. His pubic hair was exposed. It was as if there was an opposite force stopping him from going further. Candy looked at her pretty little watch.

"Daisy, we have thirty minutes, please get a move on."

David closed his eyes and tugged his panties down to his knees. His erection sprung free into the humid air.

"Oh my." Candy put a hand to the side of her face and her mouth remained in an open O shape.

His erection strengthened, hard firm, almost bursting.

"You'll need to lose your erection before we go downstairs, Daisy. If it hasn't reduced by the time you've had your bath and treatments, I'll have to think about the best way to get it done. Yes?"

David got into the bath without comment, keen to get the object of his embarrassment out of sight beneath the bubbles.

"Lady Elena told me I had to bathe you and clean you."

This was getting worse by the minute. At the same time, it might not be so bad. Ruth was downstairs. Candy took a sponge and squirted bath gel on it. She scrubbed his back. He had to admit it was nice to be spoilt. Candy turned her attention to his front.

She scrubbed his face, then his shoulders, arms and chest. David's eyes fixed on her deep cleavage, mere inches from his face and straining against a large low-cut bra. She cleaned his body. His erection strained further at the sight of her tits. He was pleased there was lots of foam hiding his straining embarrassment.

Candy scrubbed at his stomach with the sponge. She then plunged into the water to wash his lower stomach and hit against the top of his erection.

"Whoops," she smiled. "What do we have here?"

David's face flushed red and hot. Candy washed around his stomach, the back of her hand brushing against his erect penis. She pulled her hand out of the water and raised her eyebrows. She brushed the bubbles away to expose his throbbing erection.

"Stand up so I can wash your legs. And some other parts," she said. He stayed where he was. "Oh don't be shy, remember, I've seen so many penises *and* had many of them in my mouth. And other places. And I've seen yours." Her smooth face creased into a kindly smile.

David placed his hands on the edge of the bath and stood. Water and foam slid away from him. Candy's eyes washed over his slim body and settled on his streaming erection. She held it in one hand then ran the sponge over his firm shaft and around his balls. She dropped the sponge, soaped her hands and rubbed over his penis and balls again. It was an utter pleasure. She pulled back his skin and tapped around the exposed head with the sponge.

His erection strained, his desire to cum intense. Guilt engulfed him. Desperation too. This strange exaggerated woman was rubbing his penis and balls with soapy gentle hands. What if

Ruth came in? He looked out to the landing. There was no one there. They were alone. Maybe he could allow her to play a little more.

Her hand with the sponge went behind and she washed around his anus. This was wrong but so good. She inserted a sponge covered finger inside a little way. Was that necessary? He didn't care anymore.

Candy let go of his genitals, much to David's disappointment. He castigated himself for wanting her to do more. Her finger fell away from his anus and it twitched. Candy washed his legs, her hair catching over his erection. She told him to step out of the bath and to stand while she dried him down. She rubbed the soft towel over his back and front. Then she moved to his genitals again and knelt.

His erection was at Candy's eye level as she cupped the towel around his balls. She ran the towel along his erect shaft. Her cool breath played on his bulbous penis head as she dried his legs. Her lips were an inch away, open. David closed his eyes. The breath disappeared. He was on the brink but nothing was helping him over the edge.

"Stay there Daisy, I have to now tidy your legs up." Candy got up, stopping for a moment at his erection, her eyes washed over it again. She stood up. A small drop of pre-cum oozed from the end

"What do you mean, tidy up?"

She didn't answer him, she was preoccupied looking through a wall cupboard for something. What did she mean by he needed tidying up?

Chapter 12 – A Shaved Sissy

Candy found what she was looking for. She took out a palm-sized white electric razor, a tin and a hand razor. Candy knelt in front of him again, the top of her head hovering under his raging erection. His sensitive penis head brushed against a ponytail, sending judders through his stomach. Candy plugged the electric razor into a low wall socket. She clicked on a sliding button and it began to buzz.

"Lady Elena wants you smooth. She has guests and your hairy legs and arms are not a good look." She ran the shaver over David's shin, removing a long swathe of leg hair.

David stood back and the shaver buzzed in the air. "What do you mean? They won't see my legs. I'll be back in my long trousers."

"Lady Elena thinks it's too hot so she has something cooler and shorter for you to wear tonight. So your legs will be on show. Lady Elena's orders."

"So what then? A pair of shorts?"

Candy moved across. "Lady Elena is thinking of your comfort. It's a hot humid night and you'll be working in the kitchen and serving her guests. She wants you to look tidy and she doesn't like to see dark hairy legs. They don't look great."

David looked down at Candy and they locked eyes for a brief moment, his erection in their eye-line. He had to admit, his legs were covered in course black wavy hairs, he hadn't considered it before but they were ugly. He sighed and thought of Ruth telling him to stop complaining. "OK, get on with it."

Candy buzzed the shaver up the first leg, his hairs falling to the floor like leaves from an autumn tree. She pulled his legs apart to make David stand like a gunslinger. His erection remained stubbornly firm. She knelt up and pushed his erection and balls up with a delicate touch as she worked the top of David's leg with the shaver.

He shivered twice from the sensation of her soft fingers against his sensitive skin. Her gentle touch and the sight of long pink fingernails against his genitals caused a ripple of tingles in him.

Candy started at the top of the other leg. She put her hand around his erection and held it out of the way as she worked. She moved the razor up to shave the area between his leg and pubic area.

"What are you doing, Candy? My legs, not my pubic hair."

"I'm making things neater for you, Daisy. Things are changing for you." She zipped the electric razor over the other side and along the top. David had a triangular area of pubic hair above his penis. "I'll shave your penis and balls with a wet razor, I think the electric one would be too rough on your sensitive area."

David pushed her hand and razor away. "You will not. I can't believe I'm letting you shave my legs."

Candy went back to shaving his legs. "Suit yourself, but Lady Elena will want them shaved too at some time." Her ponytail intertwined around David's erection

David shook his head to himself. What has his penis and balls got to do with his employer? As he pondered the dilemma, Candy finished shaving his legs, chest and arms. David complied meekly.

Candy returned to the cabinet and took out a plastic bottle of moisturiser. "Stay there for a little longer, I need to moisturise your shaved skin with this."

It could be worse, thought David. There was something odd about Candy. She sometimes seemed clumsy on her heels and occasionally put things down in a heavy manner. These things contradicted her look. Candy squirted a huge dollop of white cream on her hands and rubbed them together. She applied it to his legs and kneaded it in, starting on his thighs. It felt good. David thought it a good time to ask where Lord James Capel-Clifford was. They hadn't seen any sign of him since being there.

"So Candy," he said.

She looked up and continued rubbing into his thighs. She was good at this and her natural lack of gentleness made it feel like a refreshing massage.

"Where is Lord Capel-Clifford? We haven't met him yet although we've been here for some time now."

Candy's hands reached the top of his thighs, her hair and the back of her hands knocking against his erection. "Lord James moved on, Daisy."

"What does that mean. Moved on?"

Candy's hands knocked rhythmically against his erection as she massaged the moisturiser into his thighs. His eyes rolled. He wasn't sure he could take much more of this without exploding into her hair. That would not be appropriate.

Her hands went under his balls and her fingers kneaded the inside of his thighs. The back of her smooth hands rubbed against his erection. Her hands raised and pushed harder into his balls. He gave out a short moan of pleasure and didn't complain.

"Lord James has moved on, Daisy, that's all you need to know. You won't be meeting him." Her hands moved over his erection.

David jumped. "No need to moisturise my penis."

She stood and maintained her hands around his erection and balls. "Lady Elena said to moisturise your whole body. She didn't say moisturise everything except your penis and balls."

David's logic told him to push her away: his sensations and emotions prevented him from moving and he closed his eyes to take in the pleasure. She rubbed her fingertips into his penis one hand squeezing his balls.

She planted a peck on the end of his erection and his eyes shot open. She removed her hands and mouth to David's disappointment. She moisturised the rest of his smooth body. The cream had a sweet flowery smell. Candy finished and squirted a perfume around his neck. She fluffed his hair about.

"It's not long enough to style, but I'll think of something. Maybe a little cap?" She told him.

Candy was seriously odd, he thought. He heard Ruth moving around in their bedroom. "Good timing," said Candy. "Madam Ruth is back. Let's go and get you dressed."

David followed her into the bedroom. Ruth was in a short black maid's dress. It wasn't as frilly and flared as Candy's, but it was short. David swallowed his surprise at seeing her that way. She looked good, a kind of fantasy figure. His erection stiffened further.

Ruth glanced over as she prepared her make-up in a mirror. Her eyes fell to his nudity and his throbbing erection. "What have you two been playing at then?" She giggled and turned to continue to colour her eyelids with make-up.

David scanned the room. He saw the empty clothes hanger, which he assumed had been holding his wife's dress. Next to it was an identical dress. Probably a spare he thought. There was no other clothing hanging up.

"Where are my clothes? Lady Elena's not expecting me to serve naked I suppose?"

Ruth glanced back and smiled. She returned to her make-up, disinterested.

"Very droll, Daisy," Candy said.

"Well," David asked. "My clothes?"

He followed Candy's stare to the wardrobe and the maid's dress hanging inside. "You are joking of course."

"Lady Elena doesn't do jokes, Daisy."

Chapter 13 – The Great Release

Ruth got up. "I'm ready, I'll go down and get things started." She left.

"I came up to see what was taking you so long."

He spun around. Annabelle was standing in the doorway. His hands went to his erection, pressing it between his legs in a vain attempt to preserve some dignity. Get into your uniform, Daisy-Flowerbud, and come down to get to work. My mother's friends will be here shortly and you will need to be serving them the pre-dinner drinks. *Yah.*"

He stared at her in confusion. Then turned back to look at the little dress, so feminine, so short. "I'm not wearing a dress, Madam."

"And why ever not, Daisy-Princess? Chop chop, get a move on. There's a good girl."

David froze at her words. His hands fixed tight between his legs.

A grin smeared across Annabelle's face. "This dress is your new uniform and you agreed to wear one as a condition of the job. Your wife doesn't seem to have a problem wearing it so why do you?"

His mind swirled. Were they expecting him to put on a little maid's dress? Ruth was watching the scene.

"Ruth, please tell her you don't want me in a dress. Back me up. This isn't right."

Ruth's forehead creased. "I don't know, Daisy, Madam Annabelle does have a point. It does seem to be a standard uniform. I didn't know the uniform would be a dress, but maybe it's our fault; we didn't check. Besides, you didn't seem to mind wearing the little skirt today. I'd say you enjoyed it."

Annabelle folded her arms. "Your wife, as usual, understands. There is only a maid dress to wear. What did you think you would be wearing? You clean, cook, serve. You're a housemaid. For pity's sake, Daisy-Petal. What else would you call your job? Come on tell me."

David looked down. The way she described it was logical. "It does sound like a maid's job, Madam."

"And what do maids wear?"

David's skin went hot. Annabelle had another point. "Maids wear maid's dresses, Madam."

Annabelle slapped her thigh. "I do believe she has got it. Now, get into your maid dress."

His head jerked up as Annabelle called him *she*. Again. Candy passed him the little dress on the hanger.

Annabelle walked into the room and swiped his hands away. "And what is this?"

His erection strained. He looked down.

Annabelle looked at Candy. "Do something to get rid of this, would you? And don't make a mess. You know what I mean." She folded her hands and stood back, her eyes on David.

Candy curtseyed and knelt in front of David. She prised his hands away from his erection and took it in one hand. David looked down at her and then at Annabelle.

"I do like to see the girls play." She tapped Candy on the back of the head. "Hurry up."

Candy's mouth went over David's erection. Her warm breath, her tongue lashed around the sensitive end. He looked at Annabelle, a wry grin a look of satisfaction. David felt Candy's mouth going up and down his erection, up and down. She squeezed the end between her lips then back over it again. Faster and faster, David surrendered to the sensations. The feelings grew and he lost himself in pleasure.

His erection jerked, a spurt into Candy's mouth. She kept moving along his shaft. He jerked violently and he spurted again. He imagined it hitting her tonsils like a rifle shot. Five or six more ejaculations and he fell away, spent. Then the terrible realisation. He opened his eyes to see Annabelle leering.

"Good girls. Now chop-chop, hurry-hurry. Dressed and downstairs in five minutes."

Chapter 14 - The Grand Reveal

"Stand up straight, Daisy." Lady Elena's crisp voice cut through the heat of the room.

David straightened, his face and neck burned from the humiliation. He was still weak from the blow-job from Candy. He prayed she wouldn't say anything to Ruth.

His hands were at his side, his little dress hung a couple of inches below his small panties. His legs were bare and smooth. He had stepped into a pair of black sandals with two-inch heels. His calf muscles had tightened at the unusual angle of his legs in heels.

Lady Elena was walking around, adjusting his dress to hang correctly, rustling at the hem.

"You need to look the part. Candy get me the cap, a pair of clip-on earrings and a necklace."

Candy scurried away and returned with the items. Lady Elena placed the cap on his head. It was more of a bonnet, black with white frills. She clipped on a pair of dangling earrings to his lobes and tied a thin silver necklace around his low front. "Much better. We'll get you there, Daisy, don't you worry."

Get me where, he thought? I don't want to go anywhere. Annabelle approached and told him to stand still. She made up his face. She brushed mascara on his eyelashes and applied a little make-up to his face. She finished with a deep red lipstick. She stood back to admire her work.

"OK, we are as ready as we'll ever be with," Lady Elena said, in her stilted aristocratic accent

There it was again, the reference to him as a her. He had no time to think as Annabelle and her mother looked him up and down. Annabelle ran a hand over his chest. She mumbled something about a bit of work there.

She pursed her lips in thought. "Better. You'll need to grow your hair long so we can get it styled better. I will look into someone coming to have those lobes pierced. Clip-ons don't cut it. And of course the breast job."

What was going on? They were planning to transform him into a girl? They wouldn't succeed. You can't turn a man into a woman. He would fight them. Ruth would not allow it. Would she?

"Do you remember the problems we had with your father, Annie?" Lady Elena stared into space.

"Yes, father was like Daisy-Popsy. He didn't want to cooperate at first. Now look at him. Almost perfect as the pretty maid," Annabelle said.

Candy blushed. "Thank you, Madams." She curtsied.

"Our pleasure, Candy," said Lady Elena. "You were never much as a man. A man called James. Such an improvement now you're Candy."

Candy curtsied again. David watched the unfolding scenario with horror. The two ladies turned to him. Lady Elena spoke. "And you'll thank us for it too, Daisy."

The doorbell rang out.

"Our guests have arrived." She turned to Daisy. "Why don't you be a good girl and answer the door. Then after dinner, you will have the special services to perform. Candy has needed someone to help her for ages now."

"What services, Madam?" asked David.

Lady Elena smiled. "Sissy housemaid duties. All those nice gentlemen guests have stressful jobs and need relief services."

David looked back at her, not understanding.

"You are a dizzy girl," said Annabelle. "Relief. Mouth relief services. That means blow jobs, Daisy. Lots of blow jobs.

THE END

Please leave me a review on the site you bought Maid To Serve

Lady Alexa

Printed in Great Britain
by Amazon